# DISNEY
## PRINCESS
### *Cinderella*

CU00842970

Published by Ladybird Books Ltd.,
80 Strand, London WC2R 0RL
A Penguin Company
Penguin Books Australia Ltd., Camberwell, Victoria, Australia
Penguin Books (NZ) Ltd., Private Bag 102902, NSMC, Auckland, New Zealand

2 4 6 8 10 9 7 5 3 1

Printed in China

# Cinderella
## A Day for Dancing

Ladybird

Cinderella was busy scrubbing the floor when her stepmother hurried into the room, waving a piece of paper.

"Drizella! Anastasia!" she called to Cinderella's stepsisters. "There is a fair down in the village today!"

Everyone was full of excitement, except Cinderella. She probably wouldn't be allowed to go. Ever since her father's death, Cinderella had been made to work hard every day.

Cinderella stood up bravely. "Please may I go, too?" she asked, quietly.

"Of course you may," said her stepmother with a cruel smile, "if you finish all your work first."

She led Cinderella to the oldest part of the house and flung open a door. "This dining room has not been used for years," she said. "When it is spotless, you may go to the fair."

Cinderella looked in horror at the dusty room. She would never finish cleaning it in time. Sadly, she went back to finish the floor before starting the massive task.

As soon as she had left the room, tiny voices were heard as Cinderella's mouse friends scuttled inside. The room was very grand and they had never seen it before.

"Look at the size of this!" squeaked Suzy, climbing up onto the table. "Whee!"

As Suzy skidded across the table, her tiny feet polished away all the dust and dirt. Jaq had a brilliant idea.

"I think it's time we had a party!" he grinned. "We'll invite our good friends, the birds, too."

The other mice looked puzzled, but Jaq shooed them back to the kitchen and told them to get ready for the party.

*L*ater, Jaq looked round the old dusty dining room with a smile. The birds had arrived, and everything was ready.

An excited squeaking was heard at the door as Suzy came in with the other mice. They looked splendid in their party clothes.

"Please put these on," said Jaq, handing out pairs of little slippers for their feet. The puzzled mice did as they were told.

Jaq tiptoed into the middle of the huge dining table.

"Music, please!" he commanded, and all the birds began to sing.

Round and round the table whirled Jaq. "Look!" cried Suzy, pointing to the table. The tiny feet of the dancing mouse were dusting and polishing as they twirled! The table would be clean and shiny in no time. All the mice began to dance.

*T*he singing birds flew up into the air.
With their delicate wings, they dusted
the pictures and the mirrors. From the
highest corners of the room, every cobweb
was swept away.

Just then, the friends heard Cinderella
trudging slowly up the stairs to start work
on the room.

"Quick!" cried Jaq. "Hide!"

Cinderella couldn't believe her eyes as she gazed at the gleaming room. Laughing happily, she watched as her friends crept from their hiding places to explain.

"Now I can go to the fair!" cried Cinderella, thanking the tiny creatures.

"I hope you have as much fun as we did!" laughed the mice.

"Oh, I shall," Cinderella said. "I shall!"